AF584304

To the most influential people in my life, my mother and father, Anne and Charles Flowers, my much-loved Grandmother, Nellie French, and my wife and children, Ceri, Joshua and Tallis Flowers. – T.F.

Omnibus Books
An imprint of Scholastic Australia Pty Limited
PO Box 579 Gosford NSW 2250
ABN 11 000 614 577
www.scholastic.com.au

Part of the Scholastic Group
Sydney • Auckland • New York • Toronto • London • Mexico City • New Delhi • Hong Kong • Buenos Aires • Puerto Rico

First published by Scholastic Australia in 2021.
Text copyright © Commonwealth of Australia.
Illustrations copyright © Tony Flowers, 2021.
Cover design by Nicolette Treanor.

The moral rights of Peter Dodds McCormick have been asserted.
The moral rights of Tony Flowers have been asserted.

The text of the national anthem has been reproduced with the permission of the Australian Government, Department of Prime Minister and Cabinet.

All rights reserved. No part of this publication may be reproduced or transmitted in any form or by any means, electronic or mechanical, including photocopying, recording, storage in an information retrieval system, or otherwise without the prior written permission of the publisher, unless specifically permitted under the Australian Copyright Act 1968 as amended.

A catalogue record for this book is available from the National Library of Australia

ISBN 978-1-76112-636-9

Typeset in Fanwood and Buttermilk Farmhouse.

Printed in China by RR Donnelley.

Scholastic Australia's policy, in association with RRD, is to use papers that are renewable and made efficiently from wood grown in responsibly managed forests, so as to minimise its environmental footprint.

10 9 8 7 6 5 4 3 22 23 24 25 / 2

Advance Australia FAIR

AN OMNIBUS BOOK FROM SCHOLASTIC AUSTRALIA

Australians all let us rejoice,
For we are one and free;

Do You
Ever

We've golden soil and wealth for toil;
Our home is girt by sea;

Our land abounds in nature's *gifts*

Of beauty rich and rare;

W
Tot

In history's *page*,

let every stage

Advance Australia Fair.

In joyful strains

then let us *sing*,

REX ROCK
Johns
Club

Advance Australia Fair.

Beneath our radiant Southern Cross

We'll toil with *hearts* and *hands*;

To make this Commonwealth of ours
Renowned of all the lands;

For those who've come across the *seas*

We've boundless *plains*

to share;

To *Advance* Australia Fair.

REMY
CAFÉ

In joyful strains then let us **sing**,

BOAT
RESEARCH
BAAA
VISIT
SA
FRESH
CRAYFISH
MUSEUM
REX

Advance Australia Fair.

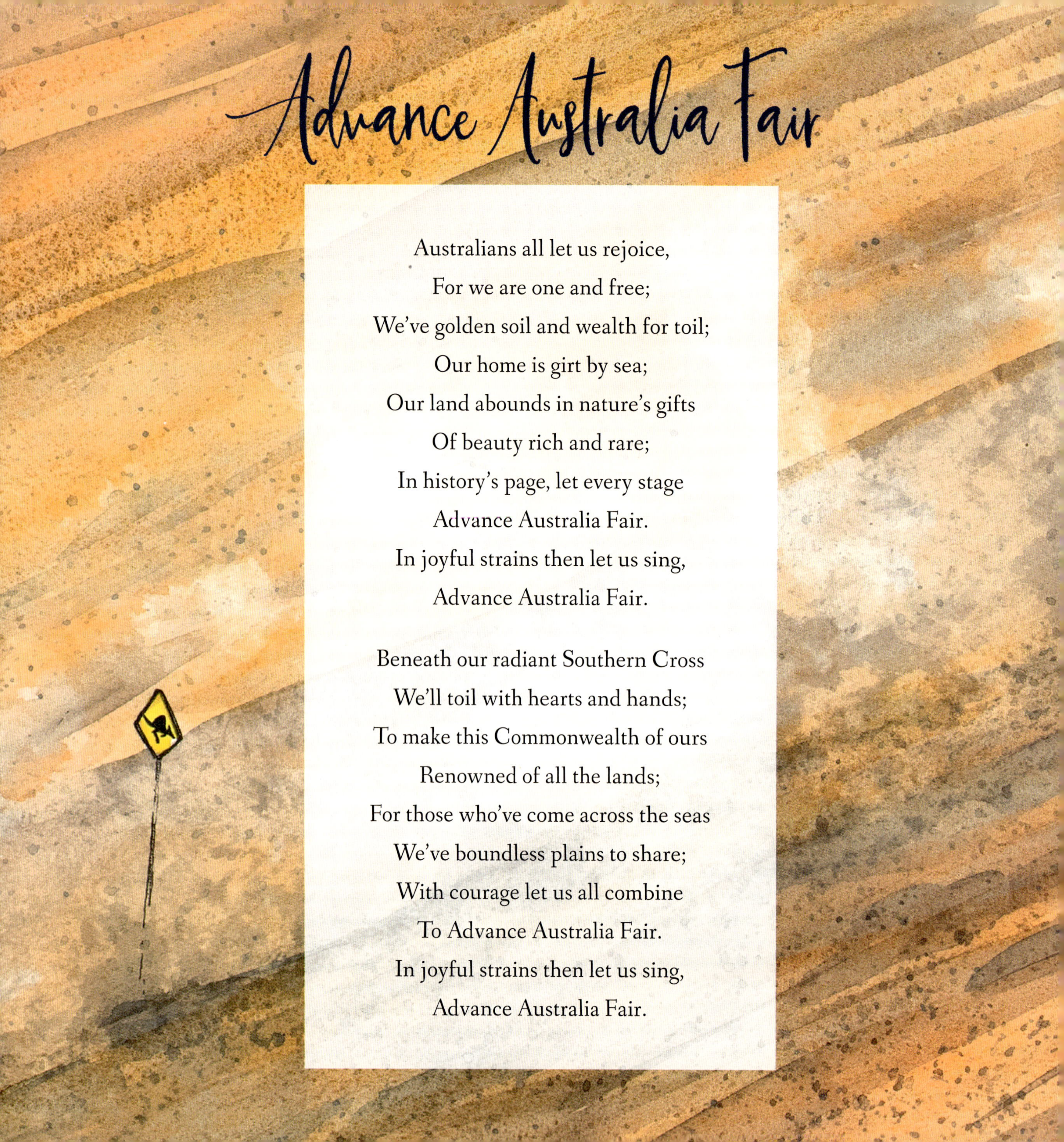

Advance Australia Fair

Australians all let us rejoice,
For we are one and free;
We've golden soil and wealth for toil;
Our home is girt by sea;
Our land abounds in nature's gifts
Of beauty rich and rare;
In history's page, let every stage
Advance Australia Fair.
In joyful strains then let us sing,
Advance Australia Fair.

Beneath our radiant Southern Cross
We'll toil with hearts and hands;
To make this Commonwealth of ours
Renowned of all the lands;
For those who've come across the seas
We've boundless plains to share;
With courage let us all combine
To Advance Australia Fair.
In joyful strains then let us sing,
Advance Australia Fair.

UHF
14
NOMADS